D0700020

PROFESSOR BRANESTAWM'S
DICTIONARY

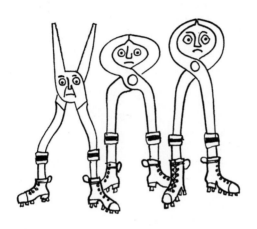

PROFESSOR BRANESTAWM'S DICTIONARY

Compiled by

NORMAN HUNTER

Illustrated by

DEREK COUSINS

THE BODLEY HEAD
LONDON · SYDNEY
TORONTO

To all the lovely children,
and their mums and dads,
who enjoy my books.

Text © Norman Hunter 1973
Illustrations © Derek Cousins 1973
ISBN 0 370 01249 6
Printed and bound in Great Britain for
The Bodley Head Ltd
9 Bow Street, London WC2E 7AL
by W & J Mackay Limited, Chatham
First published 1973
Reprinted 1973

PREFACE

Words are strange things. Playing with them can be fun, but you want to be careful. Some of the very long, curly ones are apt to wind themselves round you and dislocate your pronunciation. And some words don't mean what they look or sound as if they ought to mean.

Professor Branestawm felt it was time some kind of research was done into words like these. For instance, take the word "inventory". Now if you pronounce it as you're supposed to pronounce it—"*in*v'nt'ry"—it means a list of things. And that, the Professor says, is absurd. An inventory ought to be a place where you invent things, and you should pronounce it "in*vent*ory". So the Professor has his own Inventory, the place where he does his inventing.

And he has now invented a completely new kind of dictionary, or *fictionary*, as he calls it. It is especially for all those words that seem to have better meanings than the ones usually given to them.

Norman Hunter

Aaron. What a wig has.
abandon. What a hat has.
abate. Something for catching fish.

ABATE

7

ABUNDANCE

abominable. A piece of explosive swallowed by a male cow.

absinth. Something that makes the heart grow fonder; condition of not being here.

abundance. A waltz for cakes.

abut. A kind of barrel.

acacia. A box is present; or, this is a law suit.

accent. A chopper dispatched.

accident. Mark made by a chopper.

accord. A piece of thick string.

account. A countess's husband.

accountant. Insect who is good at figures.

accrue. People who look after a ship.

accurate. Vicar's assistant.

acquire. Group of singers.

addition. What a dinner table has.

administer. A clergyman in a television commercial.

adverse. Stick on some poetry.

aftermath. The next lesson after arithmetic.

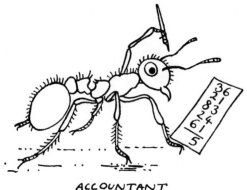

ACCOUNTANT

agate. What you count sheep jumping over, in order to get to sleep.

agenda. Masculine, feminine or neuter.

alight here. A fire at this place.

alligator. Legging for wearing in narrow streets.

allocate. A greeting for Catherine.

allotment. A good deal is intended.

already. Completely crimson.

also. Everybody stitch.

alternate. Change Nathaniel.

analyse. Ann doesn't tell the truth.

angler. Someone good at geometry.

antennae. There are none.

antimony. Opposed to cash.

aspirate. In the same way as a seagoing robber.

baccarat. Gamble on a racing rodent.

BACCARAT.

badminton court. That villainous Mr Minton has been captured.

bandeau. Forbidden French water.

barcarolle. Sailing ship wallowing in rough sea.

baton. Continue playing cricket.

benign. Be a year older than eight.

beret. What a dog does with a bone.

bicycle. Purchase a thing for cutting long grass.

BULLETIN.

bison. A thing for making puddings in.

bizarre. A peculiar shop.

boycott. Bed for a male baby.

budget. What you can't do to an immovable object.

bulletin. Container for a bossy person.

buoyant. Male insect.

cabaret. Row of taxis.

Caerphilly. How to cross a road in Wales.

candidate. Small fruit preserved in sugar.

canister. Is the gentleman able to move?

cantilever. Is the gentleman not able to go away from the lady?

capsize. How large a hat you wear.

carnation. Race of people who live in motor cars.

carpet. Dog in a motor.

cartridge. Made by a cart wheel.

castanet. Throw out a thing to catch fish.

catastrophe. Pussy has a challenge cup.

cauliflower. Kind of dog rose.

cellaret. A small salesman.

chalet. Opposite of shan't he?

chamfer. Imitation animal skin.

CATASTROPHE

COCHINEAL

cinnamon. Scottish enquiry as to whether a man has been observed. (*Have you seen a man?*)

circuit. A baby cat who has been knighted.

climax. An alpenstock.

cochineal. Secure a long, narrow fish.

commentator. An ordinary spud.

copper nitrate. What policemen get paid for working overtime in the evenings.

conversion table. A piece of furniture that folds up into something else when you least expect it to.

crank. A thing that makes revolutions.

cross purposes. Bad-tempered fish.

cyclamen. Not very healthy gentlemen.

COMMENTATOR

dairy. Has he the courage to ?

data. Make an appointment with a lady.

decoration. A speech on board ship.

Defoe. The enemy author.

deform. The class you are in at school.

dense. What a car gets in a collision.

dentist. One who makes dents in things.

dialogue. Change the colour of a piece of wood.

dictum. The two companions of Harry (*Dick, Tom*).

diploma. The man who comes to mend a burst water pipe.

disband. This group of musicians.

disconcert. An entertainment of gramophone records.

discover. Case for a gramophone record.

DECORATION

distrain. This particular engine and carriages.

dogma. A puppy's mum.

dozen. Opposite of what one does.

ductile. Material for a water fowl's roof.

during. Did you use the bell?

EDUCATION

edifice. Mrs Fiss's husband.

education. Something that takes the kids out of Mum's hair and puts them in the teacher's.

eider. One or the other.

elliptical. A kiss (*a lip tickle*).

emergency. Go out and look.

emulate. Emma, you are not on time.

enchant. A female chicken's song.

encored. On a piece of string.

endorse. Inside the house.

enterprise. Come in, award.

EMERGENCY

euphonium. Italian request to get someone on the telephone.

Europe. A piece of cord belonging to you.

explain. Eggs cooked without any trimmings.

expunge. Cake made with eggs.

falsehood. A sham hat.

FONDANT.

fanfare. An exhibition of fans.
farcical. A long bicycle ride.
farthingale. A cheap blast of wind.
filbert. Give Albert a good meal.
fondant. A loving female relative.
forfeit. A quadruped.

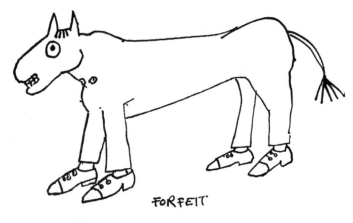

FORFEIT

forlorn. A mower.
freesia. Makes you cold.
fuchsias. Not many French cats (*few chats*).
fungi. A comedian.
furlong. The coat of a Persian cat.

gable. A jolly male cow.

gallican. Utensil from a ship's kitchen.

Galloway. She's hopped it.

gnu. Opposite of old.

grateful. There is plenty in the fireplace.

grimace. The Ace of Spades.

gruesome. Past tense of grow some.

guide. Made fun of.

handicap. Convenient hat.

hearing aid. A drink made from fish.

hirsute. Lady's costume.

history. Boy's explanation for being late at school.

humbug. Insect that makes a droning sound.

Hurlingham. Throwing things about.

hyacinth. Familiar greeting for Cyn-
thia.

HURLINGHAM

igloo. An Eskimo's toilet.

IGLOO

INTEGRATE

impunity. Devils getting together.
infer. Wearing animal skins.
integrate. In the fireplace.
intent. Camping.
isinglass. Someone wearing spectacles.

jabber. Prod the lady.

japonica. Oriental person on a motor car.

jargon. The vase is no longer here.

Joe King. The man you must be.

jorum. Chat 'em up.

Juggernaut. An empty jug.

juniper. Did you pinch the lady?

Juno. Are you aware?

JAPONICA

khaki. A thing for starting a motor car.
Kidderminster. Hoax a church.
knapsack. Sleeping bag.

KNAPSACK.

liability. Capacity for telling untruths.

lieutenant. Occupier of house or flat who is no longer there.

Lilliput. Flowering golf term.

lorgnette. A little patch of grass.

lynx. Parts of a chain.

macadam. The first Scotsman.

mantilla. Male person who cultivates the land.

marigold. Have a rich wife.

maximum. Married lady who wears long skirts.

meander. Myself and girl friend.

metronome. Pixie living on the Paris underground railway.

Michaelmas daisies. Flowers named after a film cartoon animal (*Mickey Mouse daisies*).

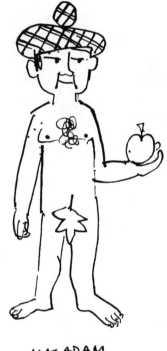

MACADAM

misinform. A schoolgirl.
multipliers. Several pairs of pincers.

musketeer. Important that one should arrive here.

mystery. Mr and Mrs Terry's daughter.

MICHAELMAS DAISIES

(*with apologies to Walt Disney*)

nautical. Badly-behaved female child.

navigate. Entrance for man who digs up the roads.

non-iron shirt. One made of brass.

noose. What's in the papers.

O

odour. Was in debt to the lady.
offal. Terrible.

OMELETTE

ALAS, POOR YORICK!

offence. A wooden barrier.

ohm. Where you live.

omelette. Prince of Denmark, play by Shakespeare.

opinion. Wearing an old-fashioned apron.

orphan. Frequently.

out of bounds. A frog too tired to leap.

oxide. Leather.

OUT OF BOUNDS.

pair of boots. Two chemist's shops.

palmist. Father didn't score a hit.

paradise. Two dotted cubes for throwing numbers in games.

parsimony. Hand over the cash.

pasteurize. Across your vision.

patent. Canvas shelter where you buy your ticket.

paucity. Town without money.

peace. For making pudding (or soup).

pepper. What you write on.

PATENT.

piccalilli. Pluck an exotic flower.

picturesque. A pretty landscape hang-
ing crooked (*picture-skew*).

pliers. Members of a football team.

policy. The parrot observes.

portrait. The charge for coming into
the harbour.

pulpit. A Yorkshireman's instruction to pound something to paste.

pungent. A comedian who makes a play on words.

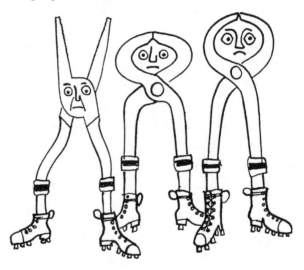

PLIERS.

quadrangle. A row in a prison.
quartering. One fourth of a circle.
quartz. Measures of two pints.
queue. Gardens near Richmond.
quoit. Absolutely.
quota. Report what the lady said.

rampage. Attendant on a male sheep.
ramshackle. Handcuff for a male sheep.

RAMSHACKLE

raucous. Uncooked swear word.

readdress. Pants.

readiness. Blushing.

rebel. With reference to a ding-dong.

recite. Put a building in a different place.

recoil. To wind a rope up again.

rheumatic. An apartment at the top of a house.

robust. A line of knitting that has come undone.

satellite. Put a match to.

Scotland Yard men. Midgets, three feet high, from north of the border.

sedate. The day of the month.

sediment. What he announced he had in mind.

Seine. A good river for nomads (*sane*).

senile. Have a look at an Egyptian river.

sentence. An order for canvas shelters.

sesame. I say, said by a foreigner.

SCOTLAND YARD MEN

settee. Lay the afternoon meal.
shamble. Imitation male cow.
signature. A little swan's autograph.
sincere. Does bad things at this place.
slate. It isn't early.

47

slope up. Lazy dog.

sofa. A long way.

soldier. Caused you to buy.

sonata. Not long afterwards.

sorcerer. Maker of saucers.

spectator. A potato with spots on.

spinet. What to do with a top.

staple. Tower of an Irish church.

SHAMBLE

SUPERSEDE

statue. Enquiry as to whether it is yourself.

Sunday school. Where they teach you to make ice cream.

supersede. Very good thing for growing flowers from.

syllabus. Idiotic public transport.

symphony. Appears to be humorous.

syntax. A fine for naughtiness.

taint. It is not.
tangent. Make a man sunburnt.
tannery. A place for sunbathing.
tea. Break fluid for people.
testimony. Bad-tempered coins.
thinking. A skinny monarch.
thirsty. The day after Wednesday.
Titan. A drunken person.
torque. Twisted conversation.
tortoise. What our teacher did.
trinket. Swallow the beverage.
Triton. See if the coat fits.

twain. What you twavel in on the wail-
way.

tyro. A line of neckwear.

TITAN

U

---

unit. You make a woollen garment.

urchin. The lower part of the lady's face.

urn. Make money by working.

usher. Tell her to be quiet.

URCHIN

variegate. Change the entrance.
velocity. We mislaid the hot drink.
versatile. Poetry on the roof.

VERSATILE

vertigo. In which direction did he pro-
ceed?

viscount. Request to Violet to add
things up.

WORSHIP

wain. Water from the sky.

waltz. Sides of houses, usually brick.

whose. A Scottish residence.

windscreen wiper. A motoring serpent; a snake on the glass.

Windsor. Did you succeed at your game, guv'nor?

worship. A battle cruiser belonging to the mayor.

APPENDIX I
Abbreviations

Language is so full of words that people sometimes find it convenient just to use the first letter of each word instead of the whole lot. This saves time and gives you a chance to catch the bus after saying them. It also saves all that writing when, for instance, you can write R.S.V.P. instead of "Please let us know whether you can accept our kind invitation to tea so that we can buy an extra bun and fill the kettle right up instead of only two-thirds full."

The Professor has therefore thought it advisable to include in his dictionary a short list of abbreviations in common use and to give, by way of variety, what they might equally well stand for instead of what they actually do.

A.A. Aunt Aggie.

A.A.A. Aunt Aggie's Auntie.

A.B.C. After Breakfast Chore (= washing up).

A.M.I.C.E. All My Inventions Collapse Eventually.

A.R.I.C. All Right, I'm Coming.

A.R.S.H. Abandoned Rhubarb Second Hand.

A.R.W.S. All Right, Where's the Soap?

B.B.C. Before Breakfast Cuppa (= early morning tea).

B.F.B.S. Brotherhood of Female Baby-sitters.

B.H.P. Best Holiday Pants; or, Bodley Head, Publishers.

B.O.A.C. Better Off At College.

C.D. Colonel Dedshott.

C.H. Commander Hardaport.

C.I.D. Call It a Day.

C.-in-C. Chap in Charge.

C.O.D. Colonel Oscar Dedshott.

C.P.R. Conjurer Producing Rabbits.

D.B.E. Don't Behave Eccentrically.

D.C.L.I. Dictionary of Choice Latin Insults.

D.Litt. Deposit Litter.

D.M.I. Don't Mention It.

E.D.C. Evening Dance Cancelled.

E.E.C. Everything Extra Costly.

E.P.N.S. Ernie Pinched Nora's Seat.

F.B.A. Free Beer Allowed.

F.G.S. For Goodness Sake!

F.R.I.B.A. For Reading In Bed Aloud.

G.C.M.G. Ghastly Crowd of Married Girls.

G.G. Good Gracious!

G.H.Q. Good Heavens, Quins!

G.P.O. Great Pagwell Omnibus.

H.A.C. Have A Cigar.

H.Q. Heavy Quadruped.

H.T. How's Tricks?

I.L.P. Indifferent Lot of People.

I.O.W. Interfering Old Woman.

I.T.A. Intrepid Theatrical Army.

I.W.T.D. I Wouldn't Try Dancing.

L.B.W. Light Blue Waistcoat.

L.C.C. Lovely Collection of Coconuts.

L.R.A.M. Lady Riding Along Motorway.

M.F.H. Mrs Flittersnoop, House-keeper.

M.L.A. Married Ladies Arguing.

M.P. Mayor of Pagwell.

M.S.M. Make Some Marmalade.

M.T.B. Mounted Trombone Bearer.

N.A.L.G.O. Nine Attractive Ladies Going Out.

N.E.D. No End of a Do.

N.H.S. Norman Hunter's Signature.

P.B. Professor Branestawm.

P.M.G. Permanently Muddled Gentle-man.

P.N.E.U. Parents No Earthly Use.

R.A.M.C. Run A Mile Cautiously.

Rev. Revolving clergyman.

R.I.B.A. Read In Bed Attentively.

R.S.M. Relatively Severe Man.

R.S.P.C.A. Ride Slowly, Pedestrian Crossing Ahead.

S.M.P. Strike Me Pink.

S.P.E. Somewhat Peculiar Enunciation.

S.P.Q.R. Send Preserved Quince Recipe.

T.N.T. Try No Tricks.

T.W.A. This Way Abroad.

U.S.A. Underground Subway to Acton.

U.S.S.R. Upstairs Shop Suitable for Restaurant.

V.A.D. Very Attractive Damsel.

V.A.T. Violently Audacious Trick.

V.I.P. Variety of Inferior Porcupines.

W.D. Wet Day.

W.R.N.S. With Rather New Suspenders.

Y.M.C.A. You Must Come Along.

Y.W.C.A. Yes, We'll Call Again.

Example of Use of Abbreviations

F.U.N.E.X.? Have you any eggs?

S.V.F.X. Yes, we have eggs.

F.U.N.E.M.? Have you any ham?

S.V.F.M. Yes, we have ham.

L.F.M.N.2.X.4.T. I'll have ham and two eggs for tea.

APPENDIX II
Late Additions

These are words that have come into use very recently and have not been put into any ordinary dictionaries yet.

meet up with. A term imported from America. It simply means *meet*.

innit. This is an English way of saying *is it not?* because it takes less time and not so much effort to say it this way. This marks the great difference between English people and American people. Although the American people like to be very quick and snappy, they use much longer words (for example, they call a lift an elevator, a path a sidewalk and a car an automobile), whereas the English people are much more leisurely and take their time about things, and they shut up groups of words like telescopes and say them in one little bite.

dunnit. English for *does it not?* See notes on *innit*. Also used in reference to detective stories, as *whodunnit*, but this time *dunnit* means *did it*.

wadda. Imported American word meaning *what a*. This is an example of the Americans trying to copy the English habit of treating words like telescopes.

waddaya. Another import from America meaning *what do you*, as in *Waddaya say?* and *Waddayaknow?* This last word really means *Good gracious!*

gonna. American for *going to*. Not to be confused with *goner*, pronounced the same, but meaning *dead*, as in *he's a goner*.

arncha. English for *are you not?* A good example of a telescope word.

APPENDIX III

Professor Branestawm's Gazetteer

Asia

Bangkok. Explosive chicken.

Hanoi. Make cross.

Peking. Taking a sly look.

Phnom Penn. Name used by an author instead of his real name.

Yokohama. Advice to return to your residence.

Australia and New Zealand

Dampier. It is not dry in this place.

Dunedin. Cheated Edith.

Geelong. An extended horse.

Hokitika. A watch for playing a game by.

Invercargill. Get into the motor, Gilbert.

Napier. Where the back of your neck is.

Opapa. My beloved father.

Tarcoola. A device for taking the heat out of asphalt.

Waitomo. Just a second.

British Isles

Aldershot. A tree killed in action.

Andover. Give it here; or, gimme.

Brighton. Clever chap.

Chesterfield. Just a meadow.

Paignton. What walls often have.

Windsor. Chapped.

Woking. Stop, Your Majesty!

Wrexham. What a rough sea does to boats.

Wroxham. What a gentle sea does to boats.

Europe

Genoa. Are you acquainted with the lady?

Marseilles. Mother goes by ship.